For Oma and Marion

English translation by Marshall Yarbrough copyright © 2022 by Penguin Random House LLC

Das Kleine Bösh Buch text by Magnus Myst copyright © 2017 by Ueberreuter Verlag GmbH, Berlin

Cover art and interior illustrations by Thomas Hussung copyright © 2017 by Ueberreuter Verlag GmbH, Berlin

All rights reserved. Published in the United States by Delacorte Press, an imprint of Random House Children's Books, a division of Penguin Random House LLC, New York. Originally published in the German language by Ueberreuter Verlag GmbH, Berlin, as *Das Kleine Böse Buch* by Magnus Myst and illustrated by Thomas Hussung, in 2017. Copyright © 2017 by Ueberreuter Verlag GmbH, Berlin.

Delacorte Press is a registered trademark and the colophon is a trademark of Penguin Random House LLC.

Visit us on the Web! rhcbooks.com

Educators and librarians, for a variety of teaching tools, visit us at RHTeachersLibrarians.com

Library of Congress Cataloging-in-Publication Data is available upon request.

ISBN 978-0-593-42761-3 (trade) — ISBN 978-0-593-42762-0 (ebook)

The text of this book is set in 16-point Adobe Jenson Pro.

Printed in Italy

First American Edition

The Little Bad Book

By MAGNUS MYST

Illustrated by
Thomas Hussung

Translated by Marshall Yarbrough

Delacorte Press

Hello! Good thing you're here! Quick, I need your help. Please! Can you help me be bad? Like, really bad? So bad that everybody's afraid of me?
That would be so cool!

I've already got a few great ideas! I'm talking really scary stories and nasty riddles. But the thing is, in order to test them out, I need a reader. Someone to play the victim, you know? Someone I can test my ideas on.

Would you maybe want to be my reader? Please? I promise it'll be fun!

Granted, you'll have to be really tough. But you're not a scaredy-cat, are you?

It's your choice, of course. I can't force you or anything. Not yet, at least.

If you're in, here's what to do:

My chapters aren't in the right order. IF YOU WANT TO HELP ME, THEN YOU HAVE TO TURN TO PAGE 9 AND CONTINUE READING FROM THERE. I'll clue you in to what's next once you get there. But if you actually are a little scaredy-cat, then you'd better just close me right now. That'd be the safest thing for you.

This is the

DUNGEON
FOR OBEDIENT

Cozy, *isn't it?*

CHILDREN!

If you want to be good and well-behaved
all the time, just stay in here forever.

Or try again on page 35!

Cool! You actually did it. You told a lie! I didn't think you had it in you. You really are a good reader. Awesome! With someone like you reading me, I'll definitely manage to become a real bad book. You know, the kind everybody's afraid of but they still can't stop reading, because it's got so many creepy stories and incredible secrets inside. Oh, and also riddles that can drive a person wild. If I can do that, then maybe one day I'll get to be really dusty and beat-up, with crumbling pages and dog-ears, and everybody will see how thrilling and beloved I am. That would be so cool!

And just so you know, we've already taken the first step! See, first I had to get your attention and get you to start reading me. That's the first test a bad book has to pass. And I think we go really well together, you and I.

But of course there are a few more things I still have to do. I'll tell you what else is coming, okay? And then you can think it over and decide if your nerves can handle it.

So, lying—that one we've done already. We'll do it a lot more times, too; that's just part of the deal. Same with nasty riddles and pranks. I think you can handle that, right? But aside from that, there are still four specific challenges ahead of us. This is stuff that every book has to master if it wants to give its readers goose bumps:

1. I have to steal something from you.
2. I have to do something forbidden.
3. I have to trick you.
4. And if I want to be especially bad, then I have to tell you a particularly scary story at the end.

One with such a terrifying twist that you . . .
I mean . . .

Well, you'll see. I can't say anything more about it here.

In the meantime, as we go along, we'll of course get up to all kinds of mischief—whatever we happen to think up. Sound good? You'll see, it'll be incredibly fun!

Or maybe you think that's boring? Well then, you're free to stop reading at any time. Although . . . well, it's not that simple anymore. Just come with me for a second. There's something I have to show you.

—⟩ TURN TO PAGE 12.

Hey, awesome! You seriously want to be my guinea pig? Sweet!

Thanks!

Oh no!

You see? Bad books aren't ever supposed to say thank you. Obviously, I still have a lot to learn. Sorry.

UGH. Apologies aren't allowed either. Duh.

This is complicated stuff. Crap!

Yeah, that's it. Cursing! That's much better. I think bad books do that a whole lot.

Crap crappity darn doggone it!

HA!

That's right, I said it.

Cool, huh? And nobody's gonna tell me not to.

Although, um . . .

That reminds me. There's one thing we need to take care of first.

So you've already shown that you're willing to go along with this. Thank—or I mean: Sure, as long as you play by the rules, I'll make an exception and let you tag along.

But I need something else, too. To be specific, um . . . well, now you have to tell a **LIE** for me.

Yeah, I know. We're really not supposed to. But I think you're brave enough to do it anyway. And it's really just a little white lie. All you have to do is confirm for me that you're old enough to be reading me. On account of parental advisory laws, child protection, that sort of thing, you understand?

It's silly, isn't it? Such a joke. As if you weren't old enough to read a little book like me.

But because I know that lying isn't at all easy, I'll give you a demonstration of how it's done.

All right, so now I'll tell you that it's not at all dangerous to read me. You won't find anything wicked or scary in me, and nothing bad can happen to you.

You see? It's not so bad. Lying won't hurt you.

And now it's your turn. You have to tell me that you're totally smart and old enough to take part in this adventure. And that you're not gonna wet your pants just on account of a few curse words and scary stories. I mean, you're not a baby anymore, right? And that's not a lie; that's the truth.

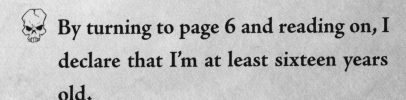 **By turning to page 6 and reading on, I declare that I'm at least sixteen years old.**

This is one of my dungeons. I've got a ton of them.

Nice and dark, right? I think there are even spiders in here.

And also, of course, **GHOSTS.**

Are you afraid of ghosts?

Do you even believe in them?

Well, if you're like most people, and you believe that to become a ghost you first have to die and then get buried under a tree at midnight by a full moon with all sorts of curses being said over you, I've got news for you. See, there's another kind of ghost as well.

You know how sometimes when people are reading a book, they say they find it captivating? As in, it holds them captive? Well, obviously, I, as a bad book, have to be able to do just that.

And that's why I've got these dungeons in me. If you wind up in one of them, that means you haven't solved a riddle correctly. As long as you haven't solved it, you can't keep reading. And then I've got you. If you don't watch out, you'll remain trapped in my pages until you go wild. But I trust that you're smart enough to find your way out of my dungeons.

Now of course I don't hold your body captive. Duh. You can just close me and go eat a sandwich or something. But while you sit there chewing, a part of you will be wondering just how the story might continue. And with that, a small part of you will always be held captive inside me—and you'll become, in a manner of speaking, a GHOST.

Funny, right? Heh heh.

Okay, so now you've been warned, at least. I mean, I'm hoping it doesn't come to that. If you wind up in a dungeon, try to escape by flipping back to the page you were on and solving the puzzle. Then you'll be free.

Hey, you know what? I've got a great idea! We can start right here. Sort of our first little act of mischief. Let's see if you can escape. That way you'll also see how it works. So have fun! . . . Ugh! . . . I mean of course: I hope you don't get so scared you pee your pants!

I will give you a tip: When you're in a dungeon, take a good look around.

Damnation! Exactly!

Sweet, right? We actually cursed, just like that! We're making really good progress. Let's go ahead and move on to the next challenge.

Now I have to **STEAL** from you.

You're probably thinking: "Sure, go right ahead, you're just a book, what are you going to steal from me?"

I didn't know myself at first. But after I thought about it for a while, I realized that there actually are a few things I could take from you.

Your attention, for example.

But luckily, I've already got that.

A really bad book could also rob you of your senses. Or your hopes and dreams. Or all your memories. That wouldn't exactly be fun, now, would it?

But don't worry. Even if I knew how to, I wouldn't do that. That's idiotic. I want you to keep reading, not end up losing your mind.

Besides, I think I can steal something from you that's far more valuable.

Yeah, really.

Actually, it's the most precious thing a person can possess. After all, even if you had all the money in the world, you couldn't buy it.

TIME.

Time is the perfect stolen good.

Never fear. You're still young; you've got a ton of it left. You'll hardly notice it's gone.

So let's get started. Do you see my faces on the following page?

Count them. But only the ones that are smiling.

The total number **minus three** will tell you what page to turn to next. But watch out! Don't get confused and miscount.

How many
smiling
faces
can you find?

Take the
answer
and subtract 3.

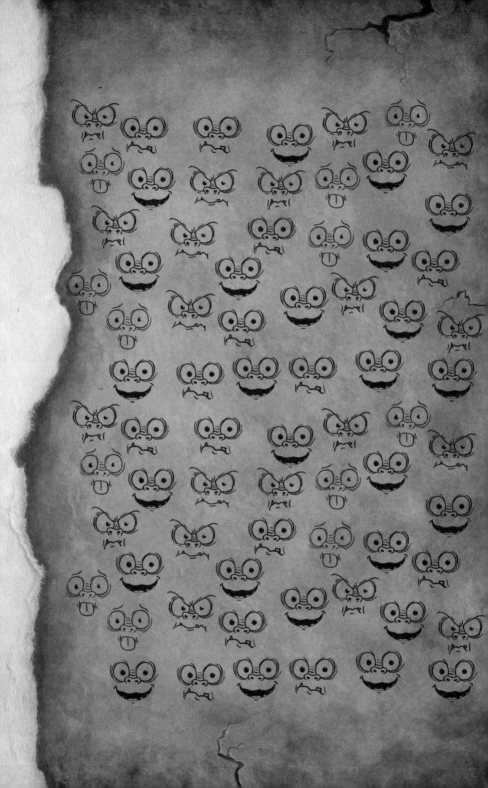

Hey! Hello! This way, exactly!

Finally someone found the clue I left. Very good!

I'm Finster. Don't be afraid. I won't hurt you. I'm a reader, too, just like you. I started reading this book a while ago, but unfortunately I'm stuck on a riddle. I just can't get past it. Do you think it's true, what the book says? Am I a ghost now?

BOO! You're talking to a ghost.

Heh heh. No, don't worry. I'm definitely not a ghost. I'm not giving up. Not this quickly.

Because you know what I found out? There's a treasure hidden in this book!

Yeah, for real!

It's not gold or diamonds or anything like that; no, of course not. It's a secret!

The book stole a magic spell! And it's extremely powerful; the book is definitely not supposed to have it. I don't know what exactly it does, but it must be incredibly powerful.

Imagine if we could find out what it is? I could finally show my big sister who's boss. And those clueless teachers, too. And everybody else!

We've just got to figure out where the book is hiding it. I'll help you if you help me. The puzzle I can't solve is on page 44. Go there now.

I'll follow you.

But I'll stay hidden, okay?

We should be very careful.

Cool. You did it!

And? It wasn't that bad, was it? Once you find out that the top half and the bottom half are the same, it goes really quickly. Or did you not notice that?

Heh heh.

If not, that's not so bad either. And you know what? As a reward for your efforts, I'm going to give you a little present. I'm going to tell you a story. It's called "The Balloon Girl," and it's about a girl named Clara.

Now, Clara was no ordinary girl, oh no. She was very

special. For you see, Clara was determined to be the most well-behaved child in the whole world. She always did what her parents or teachers wanted her to do.

Take the trash out? "Yes, Mom."

Don't dawdle. "Sorry, Dad."

Clean the whiteboard. "Of course, teacher, sir"—and this with a curtsy.

Wherever there was a sign that said "Keep Off the Lawn," "Wash Your Hands," or "Do Not Touch," she obeyed. And to the letter. If the teachers asked her a question, she always told the truth, which very early on earned her a reputation as a tattletale. Even at the dinner table she always asked if she could be excused, no matter if everyone else had long since finished eating.

One day she was sitting at dinner with her parents when suddenly she felt like she had to fart. At first she fought the urge. But then she started thinking. This was her home, after all. And she was with her parents, the people who loved her most. So why not? And so she gave a sigh and happily let one rip.

Her parents, to her surprise, didn't find this at all funny. They sat there shaking their heads, horrified. No, a good girl doesn't do such a thing. How rude. I mean, really. Surely she was old enough by now to control herself, wasn't she?

Clara turned bright red. She was deeply ashamed of her disobedience and felt like a common criminal. Amid a hail of apologies and tears she swore never to far— No, good girls didn't speak like that: "Never to pass wind again. I promise!"

And of course she kept her promise. From then on she squeezed her butt cheeks together whenever a naughty toot might dare to try to slip between them. In order to be especially good, she didn't permit herself to burp anymore. And even when she was on the toilet, she did her business only with the utmost caution. After all, she had made a promise. And promises count on the toilet, too.

True, it wasn't easy for her to control herself. But because she was so good and well-mannered, she bravely kept it up. Of course, there was no denying that her behavior had consequences. It wasn't just that she had a bit of a stomachache. Anyone who saw her noticed that she was getting a bit fatter every day. All the gas remained trapped inside her body and made her puffier and puffier. Where else was it supposed to go?

When, after a few days, her parents took notice, they wrinkled their noses. She should watch her weight, they told her. Proper little girls kept to a diet. And so Clara obeyed them, of course. From then on she lived exclusively on a diet of beans. And even if that doesn't sound very appetizing, it truly worked wonders.

For you see, she didn't get any thinner, no. The gas that the beans produced inside her puffed her up even faster. Soon she could barely fit through doors. And her fingers looked like little sausages.

Nevertheless, according to her scale, she actually weighed a bit less each day. All that gas was lighter than air. And despite her considerable girth, she now skipped nimbly over the ground. In the schoolyard she was known only as "the balloon girl." And when she walked, she looked like an astronaut walking on the moon.

Clara was happy. "Higher, higher!" she thought. "Just a little more and I'll be able to fly like a superhero!"

Then came her birthday, and Clara got to ask for her favorite dish. When her mother asked her what she wanted, she cried without hesitation: **"Bean soup with extra beans!"**

She ate the whole pot by herself. Or to be more precise: she absolutely devoured it. And that night she was so giddy with expectation that she could hardly sleep. Starting tomorrow morning, she wouldn't walk to school ever again. No, she would fly! And all because she had been especially well-behaved! But while she might have been obedient, she wasn't a dope, and so for safety's sake, she filled a plastic bottle with nails and attached it to a long rope to serve as an anchor she could use to keep herself on the ground. She tied the

rope around her wrist and drifted off to sleep, dreaming sweet dreams. She dreamt of the distant lands she would visit, and of all the people there who would admire and celebrate her.

Unfortunately, as I'm sure you've already guessed, this big journey never took place. In fact, she never even made it to school. The police were able to piece things together afterward.

Apparently, while she was filling up her plastic-bottle anchor, Clara had dropped one of the nails onto her bed. At some point while she was asleep, she must have rolled over onto her side where the nail was, and then . . .

Yep. The poor girl never had a chance. She popped like a balloon.

If it's any consolation, we can say that it must have happened pretty quickly. She probably didn't notice a thing.

For her parents, of course, it wasn't so nice. Not only were they rudely awakened in the middle of the night by a horrible bang, they also had to witness the sight of their daughter. . . . Well, it's better you don't even imagine it. It wasn't pretty, in any case; that I can tell you. And then of course there was the STENCH!

Yeah. What can I say? This story doesn't have a very happy ending. Regardless, I just have to tell it. Because, you see, I think it contains an important lesson. I mean, think about it: Here you have this super-well-behaved girl. And even though she's always sweet and always does everything right, her story ends . . . well, on the ceiling, with a loud BANG.

There's only one possible conclusion, right?

Right. Obedience isn't worth it.

And that's fine with me. 'Cause that's exactly what the next challenge is all about. We both have to be disobedient. And this story was kind of like the preparation for it. To make it easier for you. You understand?

☠ Yeah, sure, whatever you say.
   —⟩ TURN TO PAGE 4.
☠ Huh? Say that again, please. . . .
   —⟩ TURN TO PAGE 23.
☠ No! And I'm not playing along with this anymore! That was a nasty story, and it's definitely not true!
   —⟩ TURN TO PAGE 54.

Good. You can be trusted to keep your word, right? You do take this seriously, don't you?

Then I'll tell you what this is about. It was back when I was really little, yeah? One day, I saw something strange.

Back then, I wasn't even born yet. I didn't even have pages. At that time I was just a few ideas floating around in my author's head. That's the person who wrote me, understand? He's a wizard, which means the things he writes are always alive, so for example, me.

Anyway: Every day I saw new ideas arrive and start swirling around. Most of them had to do with different ways I could become even meaner, more hideous, and more gruesome. After all, I was supposed to be a really bad book.

36

But one idea was different.

It just whizzed past really quickly. Just for an instant. But for that one instant, it was crystal clear. And I couldn't even believe it. Because it was about how a part of me could also be GOOD.

Can you imagine that? I was supposed to be sweet. And nice. And, like, funny!

Unbelievable, right?

Naturally, my author suppressed the idea immediately. And I never saw it again after that.

But now that I'm thinking back on it, it gives me an idea of my own. Because if I'm a bad book and I want to be really and truly disobedient and do something totally forbidden, then I've actually only got one choice, right?

I have to do something GOOD.

Yeah, I know, it sounds weird, but here's my plan: really, as a bad book, I shouldn't ever be nice to you. That's what I was told by a few books I met on the shelf in the library. There were always these really old, thick tomes lined up next to me. Some of them even had locks on their covers or bindings made of real dragon skin.

Sick, right?

And whenever I asked them how I could grow up to be as big and fearsome as they were, their advice was always to treat my readers in as unfriendly and condescending a way as possible.

But I'm not going to do that. I think that's RIDICULOUS. If I did that, you definitely wouldn't read me. No one would read me. I have no idea what they were thinking.

But I thought: If the idea is to do something really FORBIDDEN . . .

. . . then, like, you know . . .

. . . well, we could be friends!

You and I.

I know, we haven't known each other long. But maybe we could be just a little bit chummy?

I think that would be the biggest act of disobedience I could ever commit. A forbidden friendship.

Sounds fun, doesn't it?

Are you interested?

I'm actually a very attentive friend!

I know lots of things about you, like, for example, that you . . .

💀 . . . **are very brave.** Or you wouldn't ever have picked me up in the first place.

💀 . . . **are clever.** Or you would either have given up or lost your mind a long time ago.

💀 And I think . . . Wait, no, I'm almost certain that you're **not going to just close me at this point,** no, you're going to try to keep reading, no matter what kind of gruesome things might happen.

You see? I know you that well already. Do you also know three things about me?

THREE STATEMENTS ARE TRUE. ADD THEIR NUMBERS TOGETHER AND YOU'LL KNOW WHAT PAGE TO TURN TO NEXT.

- I have fewer than 97 pages. *166*
- My favorite color is pink. *28*
- I would like to be really dusty and beat-up-looking. *1*
- I'm 8 3/4 inches tall. *20*
- I have more than 97 pages. *27*
- There's a mistake on my back cover. *147*
- I don't like dog-ears. *223*

? + ? + ? = PAGE NUMBER

MWAHA

Tricked Again!

42

HAHAHA

You've only got **one chance**
left to escape. Go back to
page 71 and choose wisely!

Hey!

You escaped! Well done!

How did you do that? It's obvious you're a super-good reader.

Oh no! Crap! That's right. I'm not supposed to praise you so much. Or else people will think I'm too nice. So . . . um, okay, how about: Hey, look at that. Guess you're not completely foolish. Better than my last reader, at least. This guy Finster. Weird name, right? Have you seen his ghost? He must be floating around here somewhere.

I gave him a little riddle to solve. Thought it would be totally easy. But for some reason he just can't do it. He even messed up his math homework because for two weeks he hasn't been able to think of anything else. Weird guy. To be honest, I'm a little afraid of him.

But luckily, you're different. For you the puzzle is bound to be really easy. All you have to do is say a little curse word. You think you can do that?

Yeah, I know, curse words are dangerous. And also totally forbidden. But don't worry. It's just a little tiny curse word. I made sure to pick a simple one. You probably even know it already.

Be careful, though. Some people are very sensitive when it comes to curse words. You'd better make sure you're alone before you do it. Put together the curse word from the letters on the next page and say it out loud. When you've found the right letters, add together the numbers that go with them. Then you'll know on what page we'll meet up next.

HU = 7

ON! = 8

MN = 1

💀

DA = 5

ATI = 2

I just can't figure it out. But I'm sure it's a
trick! The curse word can only consist of four
letter combinations! One of them is just a
decoy. But which four groupings form a curse
word?

? + ? + ? + ? = page number

Wow, you found all that out about me?

That means we're really friends now! Awesome!

Forbidden Friends, heh heh. I'm feeling super bad right now. How about you?

I'm so excited. I've never had a friend before.

You're the first reader ever to get this far. Finster didn't make it even half as far as you. And I don't think he's such a good fit as a friend, either. I think my puzzles drove him wild for real.

Well, anyway, I don't actually know how friendship is supposed to work. We don't have to dance together now, do we? Or sing?

That would be **EMBARRASSING.**

Still, we've already shared a secret. And I'm pretty sure only real friends do that, and—

Ahem . . .

Excuse me if I interrupt you two lovebirds, but . . .

This silly book isn't actually serious about this, is it? "The bad book has a good side"— that's the secret? I'll tell you what that is, that's a giant pile of whipped dog poop!

Listen, you can't let this dumb book play you for a sucker any longer. It's trying to jerk you around!

We've got to do something.

Do you have a bucket and a faucet nearby?

We could use them to force the magic spell out of it! You could also threaten to rip one of its pages out if it doesn't tell us.

That's bad, too, isn't it? Making threats. Extortion. Also vandalism. Yeah! That's exactly the kind of thing the book is supposed to be into, isn't it? Plus it's fun!

Come on! Let's show it who's in charge! Wouldn't you also like to know a magic spell that would make you super powerful? Huh?

Well, let's go, then. I'm counting on you!

What the—? Where were you? Were you gone for a second?

Oh, that was Finster, wasn't it?

Poor guy.

Is he still after that magic spell I stole?

If only he knew . . .

Yeah, I admit it. I stole the spell. It's true.

But Finster cannot under **any circum-stances** get ahold of it. A guy like him with a spell like that could really get up to some dangerous stuff.

Should I tell you what I've found out about him since he's been trapped inside me? He likes to torture insects. Locks 'em in jam jars and watches them starve or suffocate to death. And he follows ants around with a magnifying glass so he can fry them in the sun. He thinks it's funny when they start to smoke and they burst. And he likes stepping on snails until the GOOP squirts out from under his shoes.

Pretty unpleasant guy. Angry all the time. At

all sorts of things—doesn't matter what. Always feels he's been treated unfairly. He must not under **any circumstances** learn the magic spell.

Hmm. Should I tell you something?

I could probably reveal the spell to you.

We've already shared one secret, after all. Two would be even better! Then we wouldn't just be friends, we'd be actual partners! Oh yeah!

All right, let's do it!

But we've got to be careful.

You see, because the magic spell is so dangerous, I've hidden it on a secret page.

You'll find out the page number if you put three of the word fragments on the next page in the right order.

Finster already crashed and burned on a puzzle like this once before. He won't figure it out this time, either. So we should be safe.

LIBA = TWENTY

CRET = FORTY

DERLE = TWO

IGSE = TEN

OURB = SIX

? ? ? = PAGE NUMBER

You see? Sometimes by disobeying you can actually get ahead! **It's totally true.** I'm sorry that you had to read such a horrifying story to find that out. But you're not sweating through your shirt now or anything, are you? I mean, come on, I thought you were brave. Grisly truths are part of the deal. And you'll find this one pretty useful for the next challenge.

That's because next up, we have to do something forbidden. And I'll admit, I'm already **MASSIVELY** looking forward to it! I think forbidden stuff is just incredibly thrilling. Dunno why, but I'm super excited already. Or do you not like forbidden things? Are you maybe just a little scaredy-cat like Clara? One of these kids who always obey all the rules?

54

Well, we're about to find out. I've got a great plan. Don't worry, it doesn't end as terribly as the Balloon Girl's did. At least, I hope not. But I'm not totally certain, either. My transgression is a bit unusual, you see, and in order for you to understand, I have to tell you a secret first.

But you can't tell anyone, okay?

Swear.

On your honor. And on your life.

I swear on my honor and on my life that I won't betray your secret, even if someone threatens to spit in my face!

—→ TURN TO PAGE 36.

What did I tell you? Here it comes! I can feel it! Well done! The secret has got to be the magic spell that the book stole. And it's about to tell you what it is. After that, nobody will be able to stop us, ha!

Pffth. Yeah. What can I say?

PSYch!

There's no secret here.

Just a damp, dark dungeon.

Sorry.

I tricked you.

Ta-da.

Don't worry, we're still friends. But I still want to be a bad book—don't you remember? And that's why I had to play a trick on you.

I hope you're not mad. Or disappointed.

Or maybe you're seething with **rage?** Well, okay, actually, that would also be fine. I mean, that's the idea.

But fear not. Because you know what? To make it up to you, kind of, I'll tell you a story.

This time it'll be a story about pranks. I know a good one. It's about a boy named Albert. He just loved playing pranks. Whenever he could, he played tricks on his classmates, his friends, even his parents. He put whoopie cushions on chairs, he made prank calls, sometimes he even

did the one with the water balloon over the door. Often he would secretly fill a cake with mustard, or replace soda with soy sauce and watch his unsuspecting victim spit it out in a high, arcing stream. He tied fishing line to dollar bills and yanked them away when someone bent down to pick them up. And at Christmas he gave huge presents, ten different boxes packed one inside the other—but in the last box there was nothing at all. No effort was too elaborate for him. It was always worth it; nothing gave him more joy than to put one over on someone else. Every time he succeeded in playing a trick on someone, he broke out in fits of laughter. He laughed and laughed until tears came to his eyes and his stomach hurt.

Of course, sometimes his pranks did go a bit too far. Once, for example, in the middle of math class, he drove a (fake) nail through his finger "by accident." The boy sitting next to him fainted, fell out of his chair, and got a concussion. Another time, at lunch, he pretended he had to throw up. He heaved loudly into a paper bag that he'd filled with sauerkraut beforehand. When he was finished, he wiped his mouth, grabbed a spoon, and began to eat the entire contents of the bag. While everybody watched.

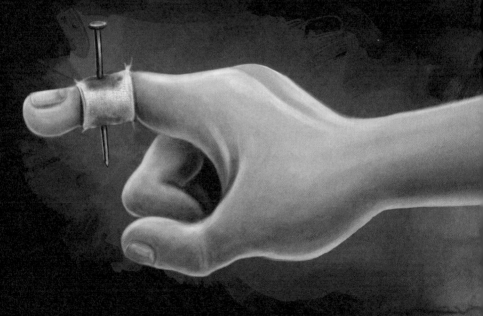

Several of his classmates threw up. Albert had another massive laughing fit.

He got punished, of course. By his teachers. By his parents. Even sometimes by his classmates, who weren't at all amused when they found themselves biting into yet another stick of hot-chili-pepper bubble gum or discovering fake dog doo in their shoes.

But none of the punishments were any use. Albert thought his pranks were incredibly funny, and that was all there was to it. The only thing that got him down was that he had hardly any friends anymore. But one day, when he was in detention yet again—this time he had crumbled brown chalk on a teacher's chair so that it looked like she'd pooped her pants—an idea suddenly came to him.

What if he were to play a prank that was so funny everyone would have to laugh at it? A prank that would make them understand that pranks weren't bad at all, they were good, **beautiful, funny?**

For days he pondered what to do. What prank could possibly be so funny that everybody would have to laugh at it? And one day, when he was lying in the bathtub, trying to make soap bubbles filled with little farts, the perfect idea came to him. Immediately he got to work.

For months he secretly stockpiled soaps of every kind. Detergent, shower gel, shampoo, old bars of soap. He used up his allowance to buy dish soap by the gallon at the supermarket. Then at home he secretly boiled all the soap down so that it would be more concentrated and he wouldn't have to carry so much around.

His plan, you see, was as simple as it was brilliant: he would try to turn the school into a giant bubble bath.

A true stroke of genius, he thought. Class would be canceled. Everyone would be let out and would be free to play in the bubbles and foam. And the best part: No one could get mad, because within a day the whole mess would go away on its own and leave behind clean, spotless hallways. Absolutely brilliant!

No one knows exactly how he managed to break into the school building at night. But once he was in, walking the darkened hallways, buzzing with excitement, he didn't lose any time. He filled all the sinks in the building up to the rim with concentrated soap. And when dawn broke, he turned on the faucets. . . .

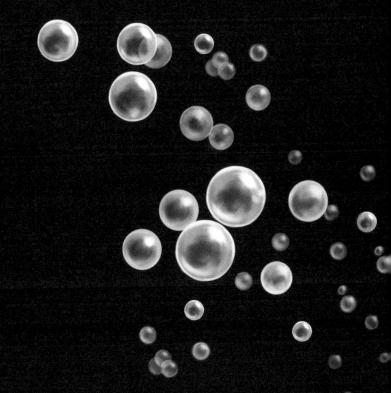

As soon as the custodian opened the doors that morning, he was immediately buried in a wave of white foam. By first bell, the bubbles were pouring out of all the windows. And when the last latecomers arrived, giant soap bubbles were rising from the chimney.

It was a spectacle like no one had ever seen. You could hear laughter and shouting. Every-

where, people were building igloos and statues out of the foam, and all the students were happy. The fire department tried to clear a path inside the building to turn off the water, but it was already far too late. The **CATASTROPHE** could no longer be stopped.

For unfortunately, Albert had overlooked something. Foolishly enough, he hadn't realized that most of the soap mixture would drain from the sinks into the water pipes. And from there, the highly potent soap concentrate mixed with the rest of the water supply.

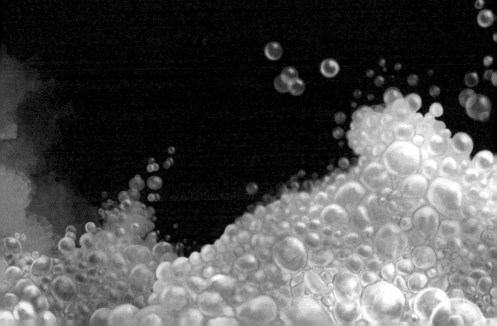

It was around eight-thirty when the first man-hole covers started shooting into the air. They were followed by fountains of foam that slowly filled the streets. In kitchens and bathrooms all over the city, people heard a sudden gurgling. Then, same as in the streets, **gigantic** jets of foam came shooting out. It filled living rooms, hallways, yards, even supermarkets. And it only took an hour for the entire city to be buried in

white foam. You could hear car brakes squealing, people crying out in alarm, sirens wailing. And amid all the noise you could also hear Albert laughing. He was certain: his prank was an absolute success.

And indeed, it was. Just this once, no one was mad at him. This time Albert was actually right. Even the grown-ups took advantage of the spectacle and used it as an excuse to take the day off. What else were they supposed to do? **It was one of the biggest foam parties of all time.** The evening news even did a story about it. Plus, in the end, it worked out just as Albert had predicted: the mayhem took care of itself before dinner, when all the bubbles burst and the foam subsided and left behind only cheerful faces, clean streets, and a sweet lavender aroma that graced the city for days to come.

But sadly, this story doesn't have a particularly nice ending, either. Because what I haven't told you yet is this: even if Albert seemed to have done everything right this time, in the end he couldn't

enjoy his prank. A prank needs a victim, you see. And this victim ... well, it was Albert himself.

They found his body that same evening. On a platform on some scaffolding. Way up high. Apparently he had climbed up there to admire his masterpiece from above. His face was streaked with tears. His body was seemingly un-injured. Only a thorough autopsy could reveal the cause of his death: the sight of all the roofs and the church steeple poking out of the ocean of foam had triggered one of his laughing fits. It was so intense that he could no longer breathe. He suffocated. He had literally laughed himself to death.

Whether that's a nice way to die or not, I couldn't say. Probably not. There are plenty of other questions I don't know the answer to, either. Was he a good or a bad kid? And are pranks fun, or more like inappropriate?

I'm afraid you'll have to decide for yourself. But maybe I'll mention one last little thing: when they finally put Albert in his grave, the whole city showed up. Everyone celebrated him, and more than a few shed tears. And even if none of it did him any good, in the end he was beloved by everyone, and many people admired him with all their heart. The boy who covered the city in foam.

So how do you feel about it? Do you like to play pranks? Or to fool people? You can think about it for a second if you like. I mean, you've got plenty of time, considering you're trapped here in my dungeon.

I have a lot of fun playing tricks on you, but hey, that's just me. And you'll only get out of here if you can figure out what face I'm making at you right now:

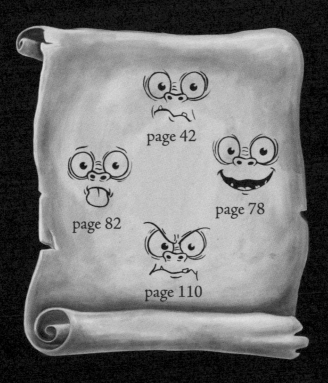

page 42

page 78

page 82

page 110

Really? You're still in?

Oh man, I could hug you!

Even though I know I shouldn't say it:

Thank you! Thank you so, so much! Of course, now you're probably asking yourself how I plan to go about it, right?

I mean, the big tomes were right.

Most of my stories do have bad endings, sure. But somehow they're all a bit funny, too. I just can't help it. I like funny stories. I can't think of any straight-up scary stories. For a while I thought I was simply incapable of doing it. And I can still remember how sad I was, because I thought I would never get to be a bad book. But one day, when I was almost finished—that is, when my author was almost finished writing me—something unbelievable happened.

I had already given up all hope, and there next to me on the desk, by chance, lay *The Big Book of Magic Spells*. The most stuck-up encyclopedia I ever met. Always turned its nose up at me. Like it knew everything, like it was wisdom incarnate. It wouldn't even speak to me. It said children's books should stay away from magic spells, said I wasn't old enough for them.

A real stuck-up jerk, am I right?

Yeah. But as chance would have it, on this of all evenings, my author had spilled a cup of coffee. And a bit of it splashed on the magic spell book. He wiped it off with a sponge really quickly and propped it up to dry. Right in front of me. It was open, and all the pages were spread out. So ... so I could see everything.

Yeah, I know. Of course it's against the rules to

copy from other books. Duh. But what else was I supposed to do? It was my last chance. And besides, there was nothing I longed for more deeply than to finally become a bad book, and here was this . . . so I just couldn't do any differently. On one of the pages I found exactly what I needed. It was a kind of magic formula. The chapter was called "The Secret of Badness." And it was about how to tell a story so scary that the reader—and now hold on to your seat—that the reader's heart might stop if they don't watch out. Especially if they're only acting like they're brave but in reality they're just a little scaredy-cat. But you're not like that, are you?

I could hardly believe my luck. This was exactly what I needed! And so I . . . um . . . I stole the magic spell.

And therefore . . . well . . .

Tell me, do you believe in magic?

I mean, do you believe that magic spells really work?

If you don't, that's good, because then you won't have any reason to be afraid.

But either way, I'm just going to go ahead and start, okay?

It's actually not at all complicated. I think the magic spell book was just trying to show off. In reality, it's really easy. The spell has three parts. Let's do the first one now. Then we'll see if it works. If not, we can skip the rest.

So the first thing I have to do is get you to read the following words:

IGNATUS SPIRI

Look at that, I did it—you read them.

So if it works, then in about

3

2

1

NOW

you'll become very aware of the fact that you're breathing, and there's nothing you can do about it.

And?

Is it working?

🕱 **Yes, I'm breathing!**

—> TURN TO PAGE 91.

🕱 No, not yet.

—> TURN TO PAGE 72.

That answer was

N.G.

Are you going to give up and be trapped here **forever?**

Or will you give it another try on page 71?

Cool. So did this work, too?

It actually looks like it's going to swallow you? Even though it's just a printed image that can't ever change?

Oh man.

Wild!

Okay, so now we have to act really quickly.

On to the last part of the spell.

This is the part where you could die.

So be careful, okay?

This time I'm supposed to gain control of your heart, you see.

The spell's instructions say that I have to tell you a story. But not an ordinary story. It's so suspenseful that by the end your heart will be beating so fast it could BURST if it isn't strong enough.

It's probably best if you lie down beforehand so you don't faint and hit your head. Just in case. I wouldn't want you to hurt yourself.

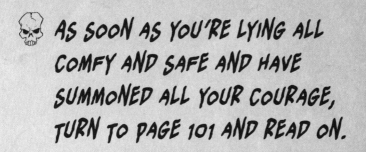 AS SOON AS YOU'RE LYING ALL COMFY AND SAFE AND HAVE SUMMONED ALL YOUR COURAGE, TURN TO PAGE 101 AND READ ON.

You see? I knew you could do it.

You really are the **best reader** I've ever had.

Yeah, I know, I was trying not to praise you so much. But we're almost at the end. And this is probably my last chance to do so. That's because . . . can you remember what's coming now?

Exactly. The last test. **The big surprise.**

And it's . . . well, let's just say: prepare yourself.

You know, way back when I wasn't quite finished yet and my author would always stick me in his magical library at night to let my ink dry, I often got to talking with the thick tomes next to me. And they told me that if I ever wanted to be like them—that is, fearsome and frightening—then that meant that at the end I'd have to do something really **BAD.** Kind of like a grand finale. And they didn't mean just a harmless prank; no, no, they meant something really ghoulish. After all, everybody knows the worst always comes at the end.

The Compendium of Contempt—that was the one with the rusty lock on its cover—finally said that for a little pocket book like me to truly be feared, there was really only one thing I could do: I would have to do the baddest thing a book could ever do. And of course I immediately wanted to know what that was.

But no matter how much I begged and pleaded, they just wouldn't tell me.

The whole time they acted like they themselves didn't know what it was, and also like you weren't even allowed to talk about it. But I wouldn't drop it. Night after night, I kept on asking. And finally, when I was so angry at how mean they were being to me that I was almost in tears, finally the monster manual next to me with the binding made of green dragonhide told the others they shouldn't be so mean. It was all right, it said. I was just a harmless children's book, anyway. Surely I wouldn't be able do any major damage.

And then they told me. Yep. They got very quiet and would only speak in a whisper. They said that the BADDEST thing a book could ever do was something really incredible:

It has to tell such a terrifying story that all of its readers feel their hair standing on end. That they get goose bumps and their toes curl. Their hair has to turn gray with horror and they have to be so frightened that they scarcely dare turn the page. Shivers have to run down their spine, their teeth have to chatter, and . . . brace yourself: the story has to be so horrifying that the readers could even fall down dead because their hearts can't bear the fright.

When I heard that, I got goose bumps all over my binding. Just the thought of it! I felt all my pages curling. And when the big books saw that, they all laughed and said very nicely that I shouldn't be afraid. Because first of all, I wouldn't know a story like that anyway. And second, and much more important: even if I did know one, a little children's book like me wouldn't dare tell it.

Pshh. Yeah.

Well?

What do you think?

Should we show them what we can do? I mean, you did say you were brave. Are you on board? Because I've got one of these stories! Before I explain it all to you, though, I have to know if I can rely on you.

And so, because we're friends, I'll give you the chance to take off right now. It's all right. I would totally understand.

True, I wouldn't get to become a real bad book, but at least nothing would happen to you. And I mean, that's what's most important.

Well? I'll ask you one last time: Would you still like to help me become a bad book, even if it means reading the scariest story of all time?

This is too much for me. I give up!

—> CLOSE THIS BOOK AND SET IT ASIDE FOREVER.

Sure, I'm in—after all, we're friends!

—> TURN TO PAGE 72.

Hey! Awesome! You found my secret message!

Quick. We have to hurry. Before Finster finds us.

I have a plan. I'll act like I'm telling Finster the end of the story. We already practiced lying. I'll do just fine.

But you have to help me. You have to read along. So he doesn't get suspicious. I just hope your heart can handle it. But there's something else that you need to watch out for. You cannot **under any circumstances** try to solve the riddles. In the magic spell book, it said that they drive every person who spends too long trying to figure them out wildly foolish.

So be super careful. You're about to read an **extremely dangerous** story. The only thing you should be thinking of is saving your own skin. Now I'll tell you how to escape from this horror story: *FIND ALL THE NUMBERS IN THE STORY AND ADD THEM TOGETHER. JUST NOT THE PAGE NUMBERS.* Finster will never figure that out. We'll meet up afterward. Oh no, we have to stop, here he com— So THIS is where you two have been hiding! You can't get away from me. Let's go! You're all out of options. Tell me the end of the story. What did the boy's imagination show him?

Can you let my reader go, at least? You don't need them anymore.

Do you think I'm going to pass up watching that bozo's heart burst? It's bound to be a complete bloodbath. That, I have to see. They're coming, and they're reading. Every word. Period.

Besides, they're definitely much too curious to stop now, right?

Ha. I knew it.

All right, I guess we have no choice. DON'T READ! RUN!

No more tricks. Start the story!

Okay, Finster, you win. The end of the story is on page 94.

Hey, **sweet,** so it really does work!

So the deal with the magic spell is that I get more and more control over you as we go through the three different steps. First your **breathing.** Then your **mind.** And finally your **heart.** That way the story at the end can have a particularly good impact.

All right, now I can influence your breathing. **Awesome.** Let's proceed to your mind.

So that's it! Of course! You see? I was right!

The book stole the secret of badness. A magic spell that enables you to instill fear and horror into everyone you meet!

Oh man, I knew it! If I learned it, no one could stop me! Everybody would fear me!

But I'm going to be quiet now. That way the book won't notice I'm here. Stick with it! You absolutely have to find out all three parts of the spell!

. . . won't have a chance. Let's just give it a try. The second part is completely harmless.

I just have to get you to look into the **HYPNO-EYE**. That's what the drawing to the right is called. No idea why. If you look at it, I'll gain control of your powers of reason. The spell book said that it grants access to your brain. Kind of like the password for a computer. Once it starts working, it'll look like it's getting bigger and bigger and is about to swallow you up.

Don't believe me?

Then go ahead and look. It doesn't take long for the effect to grab hold of you:

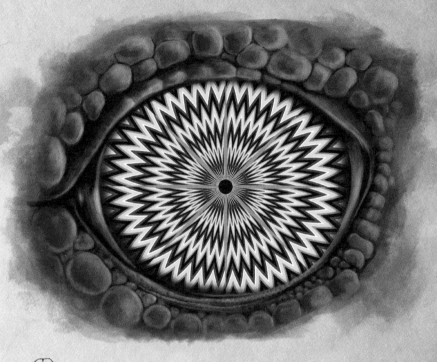

💀 **You're right! It's trying to swallow me!**
→ *TURN TO PAGE 80.*

💀 **I don't see a thing.**
→ *TURN TO PAGE 91.*

The girl went pale and pointed behind him: "Too late. Here it comes."

The boy was frozen with fear. But he couldn't help it. It was like an invisible hand had seized hold of him—he turned around. And then he saw that . . .

Come on, out with it already!

Ahem, uh, so then he saw a small green cater-pillar crawling toward him on the floor.

What?! A caterpillar isn't scary! What do you think I am, foolish? **Tell the story right!**

No, honest, it was a caterpillar. And it smiled and asked in a squeaky child's voice: "If **three** trees fall in the forest and no one is there to hear them, do they make a sound?"

Huh? What a silly question. If no one is there, then . . . um . . .

Then the caterpillar started to grow. It became as big as a snake. On its back were **seven** dark spots. And suddenly, a single long, sharp poison tooth came jutting out of its mouth.

The caterpillar giggled and asked, lisping on account of the poison tooth:

If I'm always LYING, does that

If it's always lying? Then it never tells the truth. But then that means that sentence isn't true, either. Hmm. What does it mean?

The fat caterpillar kept growing. It crawled ever faster toward the boy. The black spots turned into thick boils with slime oozing out of them. A second poison tooth came poking out of its maw. Crooked and curved, it jutted out menacingly, and slobber dripped onto the floor. Now the girl was cowering behind the boy. "You sure imagined a terrifying creature," she whispered fearfully.

The caterpillar's breath was heavy and rasping. Something was moving under its skin. As if there was something in there that was trying to come bursting out.

Oh yeah, I can feel it, here it comes! It's about to transform! This is so sick!

Then the caterpillar spoke in a deep rasping voice: "If the moon is reflected in a graveyard puddle **45** inches wide and **45** inches across at **twelve** noon, how many stars shine within?

Now the caterpillar looked at him with glowing red eyes. "I'm waiting for your answers. As soon as you give them to me, the metamorphosis will be complete."

Okay, I can handle this, no problem.
So if a tree falls and no one's there . . .
hmm . . . But there's always someone there, right? Bacteria, at least. Do bacteria have ears? But if the caterpillar is always lying, maybe it means the other way around.

Exactly! The moon doesn't shine at noon, it only shines at night. Or is it maybe talking about the sun? The sun is a star, too!

Ha! I'll figure it out, just wait!

I can handle this!

I can handle anything!

I'm invincible!

Are you lying comfortably? Are you **sure** you're
ready for this?

Okay, good. Then let's get started:

There once was a boy who was supposed to
go to sleep. But he didn't want to, because he
was reading a particularly suspenseful book. He
read and read. And when his father came in
and angrily turned off the light, he pulled the

covers over his head and secretly kept reading with a flashlight.

Because this book was different.

Different from all the other books he'd ever read. It was like it was talking to him. Like it knew him, even. And one day, when he got to a particularly suspenseful spot, the book said suddenly: "I think I can hear your heart pounding. You're not scared, are you?"

The boy shook his head. He wasn't. What was he supposed to be scared of? He just wanted to know what happened next.

"But I can hear it pounding," the book continued. "Thump ... thump ... thump ... Don't you hear it?"

The boy stopped for a second and listened, trying to hear his own heart beating. But there was nothing. And he wasn't scared, either. Or well, only a little tiny bit.

"Well, that's strange," said the book. "I was sure I... There! There it is again. Something's out there!"

The boy gave a start. This time he had heard it, too.

There was a thumping sound. In his room!

Then, suddenly, there was a quiet SCRATCH-ING noise.

Then it was quiet again.

Now the boy could hear his heart pounding after all. And goose bumps spread all over his back.

"There's something out there," whispered the book.

Again there was a scratching sound. Louder this time. Like claws digging into the desk.

Then all of a sudden they heard a second sound from the other side of the room. A deep GROWLING sound.

"Now at least we know that it's not just a cat," said the book. "It's some kind of monster—or monsters. We've got to get out of here!"

The boy didn't believe in monsters. But it really didn't sound like a cat. His heart was racing. He could hear it pounding in his ears. The book was right. They had to get out of there. And as quickly as possible. He thought for a second, then decided to just make a break for it. If he ran fast enough, he might be able to catch the monsters off guard and give himself time to slip out the door. And so he gathered all his courage, leapt out from under the covers, and ran as fast as he could.

He didn't get far. When he threw off the covers, he saw that his whole room was wreathed in a blue glow. Frightened, he stumbled and fell headlong to the floor. When he came to his senses again, he was looking into the eyes of a

grinning skull. A little spider was perched on top and said, with a curious look in its eyes, "Hello." The boy screamed loudly and looked around in horror. There were bones scattered all around him! Some of them even looked human! What was going on here? His heart was pounding like mad.

BOOM BOOM. BOOM BOOM. BOOM BOOM.

He tried to pick himself up, but it was too late. A hand suddenly grabbed him from behind. He spun around and saw a beautiful girl. She smiled and said, "Don't be afraid. I'm just your imagination. The book that you're reading awakened me."

Just his imagination? So none of this was real? He didn't need to be afraid? The boy let out a sigh of relief. Then the girl smiled at him again and asked: "Should I show you the most horrifying thing you could ever imagine?"

The boy froze and vehemently shook his head. But the girl went pale and pointed behind him: "Too late. You already thought of it. Here it comes."

The boy was frozen with fear. But he couldn't help himself. It was like an invisible hand had seized hold of him—he turned around. And there he saw that . . .

So, he saw . . .

There he saw that . . .

. . .

Oh, I just can't do it! I can't tell you the end. Crap!

I'm too afraid that I might kill you.

I mean, we're friends!

How am I supposed to . . . ?

I just can't manage to . . .

Darn. The big books were right.

Oh, you cannot be serious!
You ridiculous book!
Come on, out with it already!
What did he see?! I want to know!

Finster, is that you? Cut it out. Go back to your cell!

You can't tell me what to do. I'll speak whenever I want to, and you can't do a thing about it. I'm stopping this story right now.

And it's not going to continue until you reveal
what the boy saw!

You can't do that!

Oh, you'll see.

And you, too, dear reader.

At first I thought I could trust you. But
then you actually became friends with this
ridiculous book. Oh brother.

But please. Do whatever you want. See
what good your oh-so-wonderful
friendship does you. You're going to stay
trapped here until the book tells the end
of the story. And then you're going to read
every word of it. Letter for letter. Until the
bitter end. Until your heart explodes
and I learns the secret. Soplus all right, let's
go. I'm listeningso.

You **have** to concentrate.

If you don't, you'll be trapped here.

Forever

ev

ever . . .

ever

ever

ever

er

captured.

Go back to page 71. I'll give you
one last chance.

Did it work?

Is Finster trying to solve the riddles?

Then . . .

Yeaaahhhh!

That means he can't try to hurt us anymore! That means we won!

Oof. Man, that was close. Good thing you played along so well.

I'm really sorry things had to get so out of hand. I hadn't planned on it.

But it would have been bad if he'd found out the whole story. Who knows what somebody like Finster would have done with that kind of knowledge? I mean, he's straight-up BAD.

Hmmm . . .

Do you think that when it comes down to

it, being bad might not be such a good thing? I wouldn't want to be like Finster, I know that much. No, definitely not.

Could being bad make you like that?

Nah. No way. What a crock! It was fun, wasn't it?

Well, I thought it was awesome, at any rate. There was that time I tricked you, and then that other time when we became forbidden friends. I thought that was funny. And then the way we worked together to trap Finster, that was also cool. And suspenseful!

But I draw the line at deadly horror stories. Seriously now.

Do you think the books on the shelf might have been trying to play a trick on me? Maybe they were just messing with me? They never would have expected me to steal the spell from the magic book and tell such a dangerous story!

Well, you just wait. I'll get back at them. You'll see. I'll think of something that'll turn me into a real bad book yet. Watch out!

But it'll probably be a while before that happens.

They'll probably give me a hard time about it. **Whatever.** What title are they going to give me now?

Maybe *The Cowardly Book?* Or *The Adorable Book?*

Maybe they'll print a sweet little unicorn and a rainbow on my cover and stick me in a pink dust jacket?

Oh no, please don't! That would be such a disgrace. I don't want to be one of those cute little children's books. Please, no!

Could I frighten you every now and then, at least? Just a little bit?

Seriously, that would make me incredibly happy.

If not . . . well . . . then I hope you at least had some fun.

But if so, then . . . um . . . er, would you do something for me?

When you put me away . . . could you maybe dog-ear one of my pages?

Please!

Then I'd finally have one. And everyone who sees me after that would know that I've already been read once. And if other people read me after that, like your friends, for example (you can tell them about me, you know), or you maybe take a peek through me again sometime, then maybe one day I'll get to be a really beat-up and dusty tome with a whole bunch of dog-ears.

That would be so cool!

And when you put me aside a second from now, could you place me on the shelf between two other cool books? **Please please please?** So I'm not so alone while I'm waiting for a new reader?

What I'd like most is if we could see each other again. Like maybe on a day when you have no idea what to do and you're totally bored. Then you could take a peek inside me. Or just flip through me really quick and dog-ear another page? Then maybe I'll tell you the whole rest of the story after all. **You never know!**

I also promise I'll never frighten you to death. **Cross my heart!**

And I mean, you know I would never lie to you.

ABOUT THE AUTHOR

Magnus Myst was born in Pretoria, South Africa, and studied film and media with a focus on script writing. He works as a scriptwriter and runs an agency for time travels and adventures, besides his work as a magician. Sometimes he is also a cookie monster. Apart from that, he is a totally normal person who unfortunately cannot stop being enthusiastic about the miracles of the universe.

ABOUT THE ILLUSTRATOR

Thomas Hussung is a freelance illustrator. His favorite things to draw are monsters, ghosts, and other fabulous creatures. Since the success of the Little Bad Book series, he has illustrated a number of children's books.

ABOUT THE TRANSLATOR

Marshall Yarbrough is a writer, translator, and musician. His recent translations from German include Ulla Lenze's *The Radio Operator* and Wolf Wondratschek's *Self-Portrait with Russian Piano*. He lives in New York City.

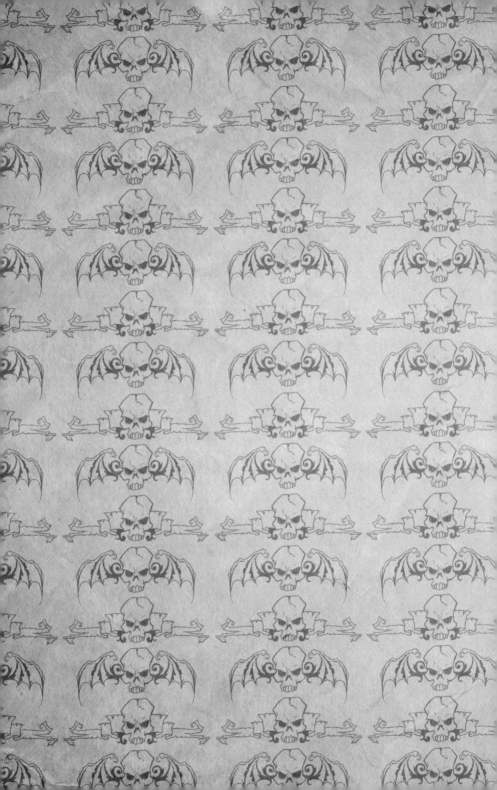